HAUNTED STATES
of
AMERICA

GHOSTLY

REUNION

D0173785

Book design by Sarah Taplin
Illustrations by Maggie Ivy

Published in the United States by Jolly Fish Press, an imprint of North Star Editions, Inc.

First Edition
First Printing, 2018

This is a work of fiction. Names, characters, places, and incidents are either the product of the author's imagination or are used fictitiously, and any resemblance to actual persons living or dead, business establishments, events, or locales is entirely coincidental.

Library of Congress Cataloging-in-Publication Data (pending)
978-1-63163-208-2 (paperback)
978-1-63163-207-5 (hardcover)

Jolly Fish Press
North Star Editions, Inc.
2297 Waters Drive
Mendota Heights, MN 55120
www.jollyfishpress.com

Printed in the United States of America

HAUNTED STATES
of
AMERICA

GHOSTLY
REUNION

THOMAS KINGSLEY TROUPE

Illustrated by Maggie Ivy

JOLLY
FiSH
PRESS

Mendota Heights, Minnesota

CHAPTER 1

UNCLE STEWART'S CABIN

Robby Warner stood at the edge of Viridian Lake and swatted another rock into the water with an old baseball bat. He watched it sail across the green water before it landed with a *sploosh* thirty yards away. He bent down to snatch up another rock from the dirt.

It was a perfect Fourth of July weekend in Minnesota. The sun was high in the sky, there were only a handful of clouds floating by, and the mosquitoes weren't too bad. Robby knew it was early yet and things could change in a matter of hours.

He peered at some of the other cabins sitting along the lake's edge. There were boats tied to the docks, a pair of ATVs parked near a tool shed, and a middle-aged man in shorts throwing a big log onto a bonfire. Farther off, someone was setting off some fireworks. Robby looked down at his swim trunks and shook his head. Instead of batting the rock, he made a side-armed throw, making it skip twice before it sunk to the murky bottom.

"You're not going to actually swim in that green sludge, are you?" a girl's voice asked from behind. "Because that I'd like to see."

It startled Robby at first as he'd never even heard her approach. But he immediately knew who it was by the tone of her voice.

Robby turned around to see his cousin Michelle standing on the grass, arms folded. She squinted in the sun, waiting for her answer.

"Ten thousand lakes in the state of Minnesota," Robby said. "And Uncle Stewart has a cabin on one that we can't even swim in. Perfect."

Michelle looked back at the tiny cabin and shrugged.

"If it makes you feel any better, I'm not sure where everyone is going to sleep, either," she said. "I think there's only the one bedroom and a couch in there. They didn't really plan this out very well."

"Really?" Robby replied. "Where *are* we all supposed to sleep?"

"Tents, I guess," Michelle said and waved her hands across the large, patchy areas of grass. "Lots and lots of tents."

Maybe I can talk my parents into renting a room somewhere in town, Robby thought.

He watched as another car pulled in front of his uncle's cabin; cars were packed in, one after another on the plot of land his uncle owned. Their family was huge, and he knew it was going to be crowded in no time at all.

A long holiday weekend in Hibbing, Minnesota, Robby thought. *With more Warners than I can count on two hands.*

A light blue minivan pulled up next to his Aunt Veronica's pickup truck. The side door opened and a young kid with jet black hair tumbled out. As soon as he looked up, he caught sight of Robby and Michelle.

"Oh, great," Michelle said. "He already found us."

Robby smirked at Michelle's comment and tried to put on his best smile as his cousin Ty ran across the weedy property toward them. He was grinning from ear to ear as he got closer to them.

"He keeps smiling like that and he's going to end up with bugs in his teeth," Michelle said.

"Guys!" Ty exclaimed. "We've been driving for almost five hours! Who's ready for a swim?"

Michelle looked down at the ground as if to let Robby handle that one.

"Hey Ty," Robby said. "Well, I was, but Uncle Stewart

says it wouldn't be a really good idea to swim. The water is . . . a bit gross."

Ty's smile faded as he looked at what Robby was talking about. There was a thick layer of green scum across the top of the water. Weeds poked up just past the surface and there was no denying it, Viridian Lake had a pretty strong fishy odor to it.

"Oh," Ty said. "Well, that stinks."

"You're not kidding," Michelle added.

The three of them stood and watched as their aunts, uncles, and much older cousins gathered around exchanging hellos and hugs. While Robby loved seeing his family, especially Michelle who lived in South Dakota, he kind of wished his dad wasn't the baby out of a family of twelve. There weren't any other cousins his age. Michelle was eleven and Ty was ten. Even though Robby would turn thirteen in September, the next oldest cousin to him was in her mid-twenties.

Robby and Michelle both liked Ty well enough. It's just that Ty tended to be a little bit of a troublemaker, had no filter and always said the first thing that came to mind, and tried a little too hard to impress his "older" cousins. Still, knowing Michelle and Ty were his best bet for companionship over the long weekend, Robby knew the three of them would probably stick together, like it or not.

"No big deal, I guess," Robby said. "I'm sure we'll find something else to do."

He looked over at the small deck running along the back of the cabin and saw his dad waving him over. If Robby didn't know any better, he could swear he was being summoned to say hi to all the newest arrivals.

Please, please tell me we can find something else to do.

But first, he had to change out of his swimming trunks, especially since he wouldn't need them after all.

Aunts, uncles, and cousins, some of whom he hadn't seen since he was too little to remember, hugged Robby, asked him how his baseball season had been, and bombarded him with questions about school. It got to the point where he almost wanted to stand up on a picnic table and just answer all of them at once. He could let them know that baseball was great, school was fine since he was in the middle of summer vacation, and yes, he had grown quite a bit since they'd last seen him.

It would've saved him a lot of time.

After Robby, Michelle, and Ty had made their

rounds, they met up at the picnic table where lunch was set up.

"I'm starving," Robby said. "All that talking and smiling. I could eat three of these." He grabbed a few small ham sandwiches, popped the buns off the top, and gave each one a blast of mustard. For added effect, he tossed a pickle slice on each before sealing them back up.

"Aunt Julie has the weirdest breath," Michelle added. She grabbed a handful of nacho flavored corn chips and a few pieces of cheddar cheese.

"She really does," Ty said, louder than necessary. "It's like she ate from a garbage pail!"

Robby groaned, especially when Aunt Julie glanced over at them, looking up from her pasta salad. He tried not to catch her eye and focused instead on Michelle's plate that she was filling up. He watched as she dropped a few cheese puffs onto her plate.

"Did you want a grilled cheese sandwich?" Robby asked. "You know, to go with your cheese?"

Michelle shrugged. "I like cheese and nothing else looks good."

The three of them found a spot at one of the many picnic tables and settled down to eat. After ten minutes or so, Uncle Stewart wandered over. Robby had watched him go from table to table as if trying to be the perfect host.

"How're you guys doing?" Uncle Stewart asked. He took a sip of his homemade lemonade and puckered his lips.

"Oh, we're fine," Michelle answered. "Robby is just bummed he can't go swimming."

"Well," Uncle Stewart said, "you could, Rob-o, but you'd probably be pretty itchy for a few weeks." He leaned over to tousle Robby's hair.

"Nah, I'm good," Robby replied, ducking away from his sweaty fingers. "I'll get over it."

"So, what is there to do around here?" Ty asked, cutting right to it. "I think we're going to be pretty bored for the next few days."

Robby cringed and Michelle closed her eyes in embarrassment. Ty, in turn, looked back at both of his cousins as though he were looking for them to back him up.

"Right, guys?" Ty asked.

Robby bit into one of his ham sandwiches as quick as he could to keep from answering.

"Oh, there's plenty to do," Uncle Stewart said. "We

have all kinds of yard games and sports balls over there in the work shed."

Their uncle thumbed over his shoulder and Robby saw the "work shed." A small, rickety garage that looked like it was two wind gusts away from falling over sat near a cluster of trees. The big twin doors in front were almost completely stripped of any paint, making it look like a black-and-white photo in the middle of a colorful world.

"In there, you say?" Robby responded. "Yeah. Okay, we'll take a look."

Stewart took another sip of his lemonade and puckered up so hard, Robby thought he might swallow his own face.

"Fantastic," he finally managed. "Hoo boy, that's tart. A little later we're going to set up the campground."

"Campground?" Ty cried. "We're going camping?"

"Yeah," Michelle replied. "Sort of. We need to put up tents for everyone to sleep in."

That didn't seem to faze Ty in the least.

"I call I get to share a tent with Robby," Ty cried, raising his hand like an overeager teacher's pet.

"Oh, darn," Michelle said.

Robby kicked her under the picnic table.

"Gotta act fast, Michelle," Ty said. "Like me."

————————

Though Robby appreciated the offer, he wasn't too interested in digging around in Uncle Stewart's condemned old garage. It wasn't until Ty asked him repeatedly if they should check it out that he finally gave in.

Since she had nothing better to do, Michelle joined them.

When Robby pushed open the small side door, the rusty hinges groaned in protest. Cobwebs tore apart and dust sifted down from the doorjamb. The outdoor light filtered in and revealed the small garage's innards.

"Holy junk pile," Robby whispered.

There was all kinds of old and useless stuff scattered about. A big muscle car in various states of disrepair sat in the middle and was covered in things that didn't need to be there. There was an old bird cage, boxes of yellowed newspapers, what looked like a church pew, and old, tattered clothes that no one would ever wear again. Along the walls were rusty yard tools, an acoustic guitar with none of the strings intact, and a series of plastic swimming floats strung onto a rope.

Must've been for the swimming area they had here

a couple hundred years ago, Robby thought. *Before the lake became a hazardous pit of sludge.*

"Where are all the games?" Ty asked. He pushed past Robby and began to poke around.

Robby marveled at all the boxes of stuff, stacked almost to the rafters. Sunlight poked through gaps in the roof, making it look like they were in an ancient temple and not some garbage-packed shed.

"Be careful, Ty," Robby said.

"Why?" Ty asked, turning around. "What do you think is in here?"

"Spiders," Michelle said, before Robby could answer. "Or rats."

Ty paused and studied both of their faces. It was like he was running a lie detector in his brain and was waiting for the scan to complete.

"Nuh-uh," he replied, then turned back to his search.

Robby glanced at Michelle and shook his head.

"You're terrible," Robby said.

"Well?" Michelle said and brushed a cloud of dust away from her nose. "Who knows what this kid is going to find?"

Robby flipped open the lid of a box and saw a bunch of magazines from the 1970s. They were warped and wrinkled from being previously wet. He guessed the roof of the garage must be leaky. More than anything, he didn't understand why his uncle would want to keep any of them.

"Any luck, Ty?" Robby asked. His younger cousin had wormed his way so deep into the garage that he was afraid the kid had gotten lost.

"You find any of that sports gear?" Michelle added. "Do we need to send a rescue squad?"

There was a loud crash of boxes and metal before Ty cried out, "Whoa!"

"Hey!" Robby said, weaving his way through the junk to where Ty had disappeared. "You okay?"

"I'm better than okay," Ty shouted back. "Wait until you see what I found!"

CHAPTER 2

BUS MUSEUM

Robby grunted as he pushed aside countless boxes of magazines and crates of old clothes to clear a path to his little cousin. He was afraid of starting an avalanche of junk in the old garage by shifting too much stuff, but he wanted to see what Ty had found. Considering Michelle was right behind him, he guessed that she did too.

After navigating through the mess, he found Ty standing in the corner, pointing at the wall.

Robby wasn't sure what he expected to see, but five different bicycles from the late 1970s hanging from the wall wasn't on his list. There was a yellow bike with thin tires and curved handlebars, a dirt bike with a big puffy seat that said TUFFY on the back, one with a small tire up front and a big tire in back, another that didn't have any tires at all, and one with a long, green glittery seat and a stick shift on the crossbar.

"Seriously guys," Ty said. "Aren't they great?"

"Huh," Michelle said, never one to hold back her excitement.

"I was thinking you found some buried treasure or something, Ty," Robby admitted. "Not a bunch of old bikes."

Ty turned around and put his hands up like he couldn't understand his older cousins' disinterest.

"Don't you know what this means?" he asked.

"That Uncle Stewart is a hoarder?" Michelle replied. "No, my mom's known that ever since they were kids."

"No," Ty said, ignoring the joke. "We could go on a bike ride. We could explore!"

"Explore Hibbing?" Robby asked. "We drove through it to get here. I think we pretty much saw all it has to offer."

Robby walked over to the bike with the stick shift and squeezed the back tire. It squished easily in his hand.

"Besides," he said, "flat tires."

"Yeah? Well, I already found a tire pump," Ty said, grabbing one near an old milk crate full of old pieces of pipe. "Boom."

Robby smiled and turned to Michelle, who shrugged.

"What else do we have to do?" she asked. "Sit around and hear Aunt Susie's dramatic bingo stories?"

Robby turned back to Ty. "Looks like we're going on a bike ride," he said.

It took a little while, but eventually they were able to extract three bikes from the mess in the garage and get them outside. Michelle decided on the yellow ten-speed, as Uncle Stewart called it. Ty took the smallest of the three bikes, the TUFFY dirt bike. Robby couldn't deny the power of the green bike with the stick shift. He wasn't sure what the stick shift did, but it was too ridiculous looking to pass up.

"We're going to look like straight-up clowns riding into town on these things," Michelle said, but laughed. "I kind of can't wait."

Ty seemed genuinely excited. He unscrewed the valve stem caps for all three bikes and insisted on inflating all the tires.

After pumping the last tire and having Robby check it to make sure it was okay, they were ready to go. They hopped on their vintage rides and pedaled across the lawn. Their older cousins, sitting around on a bunch of lawn chairs, held up their lunch plates and drink bottles. They whistled and cheered as the three of them rode past.

"Looking good, Robert!" his cousin Jim called.

"Ty, show us a wheelie!" Aunt Cheryl shouted. She

was waving her fist in the air like she was on a daytime talk show.

"Hard to believe we're the youngest ones here," Michelle blurted.

They didn't do any tricks, but instead rode past the crowd and onto Uncle Stewart's dirt driveway. The road was full of loose stones that popped and crunched under their ancient tires. The chains on the bikes groaned with every pedal push, but for bikes at least three times older than their riders, they rode surprisingly well.

"Where should we go?" Robby asked.

He was kind of excited to get some speed going and see what the stick shift did.

"Anywhere but here," Michelle said. "I mean, the farther away the better, right?"

Robby nodded. He loved his family, but they definitely got to be a bit much. He thought taking a break from them for a little while was a good idea.

They rode onto the main road and followed it away from the lake and the few cabins nearby.

"This is great," Ty shouted. He laughed as he hit a bump in the road and caught the tiniest bit of air. "We're like a motorcycle club or something."

Geez, is there not much to do in New Ulm? Robby

thought. *I know it's a small town, but just about everything excites him!*

They rode for twenty minutes before they finally rolled into downtown Hibbing. While the town wasn't as busy or exciting as downtown Minneapolis, Robby thought it was kind of cool. It felt like they were visiting a place from the past. And they had the perfect bikes for it.

The three of them turned left onto 1st Avenue.

"Whoa," Michelle said, "they have a video store! I didn't think those existed anymore."

"What's a video store?" Ty asked, hopping his bike up onto the sidewalk for a closer look as they passed by.

"My mom said that when she was younger there were stores that were kind of like libraries. You rented movies and played them on VCRs," Michelle explained. "I bet that place rents DVDs and Blu-ray discs now, though."

"Why didn't they just download them?" Ty asked. "Like on their phone?"

"Good question," Robby said. "Guess they couldn't back then."

They kept rolling through town, marveling at the odd little stores and businesses. They came across a place that looked like it had been a movie theater at one time but was now a deli. At the next intersection, they took a right and made their way to 3rd Avenue.

After they'd been riding for nearly a half hour, Robby decided it was time to try the stick shift.

"Okay," he announced, "prepare to watch this old bike take off!"

Michelle rode up alongside him.

"You sure you want to do that?" she asked.

"Are you kidding?" Robby cried. "Look at this sweet thing!"

"Do it, do it," Ty chanted. He was standing up on his pedals to give himself a speed boost.

Robby gave a thumbs up, pedaled hard, and pulled the stick shift back.

Immediately, he wished he hadn't.

The chain began to chatter and sputter on the back wheel, making the bike jerk back and forth a little. It was as if the little green antique was struggling to keep going. Robby swerved and tried to keep going, convinced it would right itself.

"Switch it back, Robby!" Ty shouted. "She's gonna blow!"

Robby pushed the stick shift forward, but it was too late. The chain popped off the back wheel and began to drag on the ground.

"Great," Robby groaned. "Just perfect."

"Pull over," Michelle ordered.

The three of them came to a stop on the sidewalk in front of a small bakery. Robby looked down at the bike helplessly.

"Well, that's the end of the bike ride," Robby said.

"It's going to be a long walk back to Uncle Stewart's," Ty added.

"You guys are hilarious," Michelle said. She knocked down the squeaky kickstand on her ten-speed and hopped off, parking it like a pro. "Jump off the bike."

Robby did as he was told and watched as Michelle flipped the bike over so that it was standing on the long glittery seat and the big handlebars. She grabbed the semi-rusty bike chain in one hand and set it onto the gear on the back wheel. With her other hand, she grasped one of the pedals and cranked it, guiding the chain back into place. The chain caught and righted itself, spinning the wheel like it was never an issue.

"Whoa," Ty gasped. "Are you a mechanic?"

"Nah," Michelle replied. "But I've thrown a chain or two in my time. No big deal, guys."

Robby clapped as if she were accepting an award and Ty joined in.

"Oh, shut up," she said and hopped back on her bike. "Are we going to keep riding or what?"

Robby flipped his bike back over and climbed back in the saddle. They continued north on 3rd Avenue until they reached the end of town. Ahead of them was a residential area with houses lining each side of the road. Farther ahead was a park that didn't look all that interesting to Robby.

"So, maybe this is the end of the line," Robby said. On the left-hand side of the road he saw a strange billboard. It featured a skinny-looking dog holding a sign that simply said VISIT ME. There was an arrow pointing farther down 3rd Avenue.

"What is that?" Michelle asked, pointing at the billboard.

"I'm not sure," Robby said, "but it's kind of random, isn't it?"

Ty slowed down behind them. "We should see, right?"

Robby thought about it. *Maybe it is a dog shelter or a dog park. Best case scenario, it's a giant statue of a dog or something weird.*

Robby shrugged. "I'm game if you guys are. We're only like half an hour away from the cabin."

Before Michelle could agree or disagree, Ty shouted, "Let's do it!" Then he took off like a bullet.

Michelle shook her head and looked at Robby. "You heard the kid, Stick Shift," she said. "Let's go."

They rode for another few minutes before it became clear where they were heading. After they passed a large cemetery on their left, they saw another sign. They all stopped to take a look.

"Hibbing Bus Museum," Robby read aloud.

The hand-painted sign had the same strange looking skinny dog pointing to the left, directing visitors toward the entrance. The building was seated in the middle of a parking lot sparsely dotted with cars. It was mostly white with red and blue accents, presumably to make it look fun, festive, and American.

"A bus museum," Michelle repeated. "Well, that's really . . . something."

Ty rode circles around them.

"We should go in," Ty said excitedly. "Museums can be fun."

Robby shot a glance at his little cousin, unsure if he was trying to be funny or not. He studied the oddly colored building.

"Are you serious?" Robby asked. "You really want to go in there?"

"Well, yeah," Ty said. "Plus, I have to go to the bathroom really bad."

Seeing as there weren't a whole lot of options, the three of them rode into the parking lot and parked their bikes near an odd triangle-shaped awning near the entrance. They walked in and were greeted by an older, heavy-set lady behind the front desk.

"Good afternoon," she said. "How many tickets would you like?"

Robby hadn't thought of bringing his wallet. He didn't have a single cent on him.

"Sorry," Robby replied. "We were just hoping to use your bathroom."

The lady grunted and shifted in her seat a bit.

"I'm really sorry," she said. "The bathroom is for paying patrons only. Museum policy."

Robby turned to the rest of his group and was about to suggest that Ty find a nice quiet place near the woods, when his younger cousin reached into his shorts pocket and produced a wallet with a Velcro fastener. He ripped it open, soaking in the exhibits and signs he could see from where they stood at the entrance. The kid looked like he was in heaven.

"I'll pay," Ty insisted.

Robby was about to decline when the lady at the counter informed them that it only cost kids twelve and under a dollar for admission.

"Three please," Ty said quickly. "I'll pay cash."

"Big spender," Michelle said. "Thanks, Ty."

Ty gladly handed over three dollar bills and the lady suddenly became a little more welcoming.

"Welcome to the Hibbing Bus Museum," she said, waving her hand toward the first hallway full of exhibits. "You're the only ones here, so you'll have the place to yourself!"

"Hey cool," Ty said, jumping up and down. "Where are the bathrooms?"

CHAPTER 3

WINDOW SEAT

Robby sat next to Michelle on a bench near the restrooms. According to the small golden placard on the wall, the bench was from 1922 and was first used in a bus station in Duluth, Minnesota. From where they sat, they could see that there were tons of display cases for them to look at.

"Seriously," Michelle whispered. "What is taking him so long?"

Robby shrugged. "Did you see how many pops he drank? The kid put down three at least."

"Don't you mean soda?" Michelle laughed.

"Who calls it soda?" Robby asked.

"We had a new girl in class who moved to Sioux Falls from California," Michelle explained. "When she heard everyone call it 'pop' she was confused."

"Soda," Robby said, as if trying it out. "It just doesn't sound right. Anyway, it's pop to me and Ty drank at least a gallon of it."

They could hear the toilet flush from inside the

men's room, followed by the sound of the sink running, then a moment later, the air dryer. Three seconds later, Ty appeared through the doorway, wiping his still damp hands on his shorts.

"You guys ready to check this place out?" he asked.

Ty walked right past Robby and Michelle toward the first hallway full of glass cases.

"I thought you just needed to use the bathroom," Michelle said. "We should probably head back to Uncle—"

"It's only quarter after one," Ty said, cutting her off. "We've got tons of time. Besides, we paid to get in here, might as well look around. Right, Robby?"

Robby shrugged. "Yeah, sure."

As much as he thought the museum would probably be boring, he wasn't in any hurry to get back to the cabin. Besides, they had two more days of aunts, uncles, and cousins ahead of them.

The three of them walked along and peered into the cases. There was a display of hundreds of miniature buses from a number of different time periods. They were all carefully arranged from the oldest to the newest. Hanging on the wall above the exhibit cases were old black-and-white photos of buses from the 1950s.

Another wall displayed items that the bus drivers wore as part of their uniforms. Big hats that looked like the ones airline pilots wear, ties, cuff links, and patches were all proudly set into the glass cases.

The featureless foam heads wearing the hats seemed to stare off into nowhere.

"Creepy," Michelle whispered.

Robby turned around from the display and found himself face-to-face with a fully dressed bus driver. He cried out in surprise.

"What the—" Robby shouted, then started laughing once he saw it was a harmless mannequin. "This guy is even creepier."

Ty walked over and peered up at the plastic dummy. A large dark hat covered its unblinking eyes. The mouth of the mannequin was set in a straight line as if it didn't think being called "creepier" was the least bit funny.

"Whoa," Ty said. "He's pretty cool."

"Sure," Michelle said. "Until he starts moving on his own."

Ty turned and gave his cousin a dirty look. "I'm ten," he said. "Not four."

"I don't know," Michelle said. "Robby's older than both of us and he screamed."

"It wasn't a scream," Robby replied. "I just got, you know, startled."

They walked along and saw what looked like wooden wardrobes displaying complete uniforms and how they'd changed from decade to decade. A hallway with bus seats was set up so that people could sit down and watch a little movie about how Hibbing bus lines got its start. As Ty walked between the seats, the show started automatically.

Ty jumped and turned around quickly to walk out.

"Don't want to watch the video, Ty?" Robby asked.

"Nope. I'm good," Ty replied.

As they continued through what seemed like countless pictures and descriptions of how the company began and grew, old music from the era was piped in through the speakers.

"Where are all the buses?" Ty asked as he rounded the corner. "Don't you think there should be—" He stopped short and gasped.

Robby followed to see what caught Ty by surprise. In a giant indoor garage attached to the museum were at least fifteen buses, parked next to one other. They looked old, with big bumpers, lots of shiny steel, and different paint jobs.

"There are your buses," Michelle said. "So, can we get going now?"

Ty ignored her and walked into the garage. Some of the buses had their doors open, as if welcoming people to climb aboard and explore. Others were cordoned off with blue ropes to let visitors know they were off limits.

Robby peeked into a couple and Ty went in and out of the ones that weren't roped off.

The three of them walked between two buses from the 1960s and emerged to find a large display of mannequins standing in line. It looked like they were waiting to climb aboard. Robby studied the clothes they were wearing. Some of them looked like soldiers clothed in their military dress uniforms.

Are they supposed to look like they are being shipped off to war? Or maybe to a training camp?

He also noticed that that particular bus was roped off to keep visitors from climbing aboard.

"So, what's spookier than one dummy just standing in the middle of a room?" Michelle asked.

Before anyone could say anything, she answered her own question.

"Seven dummies," Michelle said. "All standing around waiting to get on a bus that's never going to go anywhere."

"You don't know that," Robby said. "Maybe when the museum is closed, they all go on a joyride through Hibbing."

Both Michelle and Ty shot Robby a look.

"If I get nightmares, I'm throwing you in the lake," Michelle said. "I don't care how green and gross it is."

Ty disappeared down another aisle of buses and Robby nodded to a small, boxy cartoonish-looking character made out of plastic. It was a little bus with big googly eyes. He held up a sign that said HEY KIDS! I'M TOOTY! The eyes looked like they were battery operated and used to move around at one time.

Now the eyes were motionless, likely stuck in that position for decades.

Robby peered through a door near the corner of the garage. It looked like a small hallway. Inside was a cardboard cutout of a bus driver who was all smiles and waving. He had a word balloon over his head that said THANKS FOR VISITING.

"Here's the good news," Robby said and nodded toward the door. "I think we're almost at the end of the line."

"Was that a bus joke?" Michelle asked.

"Maybe," Robby said, smirking.

As Robby and Michelle stood there waiting for Ty, Robby looked at the bus with the mannequins lined up in front of it. A moment later, one of the bus windows slid up and clicked shut.

"Did you see that?" Robby asked.

"Yeah," Michelle said. "Maybe it was Ty?" It was more of a question; she didn't sound convinced.

Just then there was the sound of squeaky sneakers on the tile flooring. A second later, Ty appeared behind them.

"Right here, guys," Ty said. "What's up?"

Robby felt his heart quicken. *How did that window close?*

"Hello?" Robby called. He didn't want to get closer to the bus, but found his legs moving in that direction anyway. In a matter of steps, he was standing right next to the crowd of mannequins. He tried to peer into the bus from where he stood. The side window glass was in partial shadow, which made it difficult for Robby to see inside.

"What happened?" Ty asked. "Why do you guys look so funny?"

"One of the windows closed by itself," Michelle whispered.

"We don't know that for sure," Robby said. "Maybe there's a—"

"We both saw it!" Michelle cried in protest, interrupting him.

"I'll go check," Ty said. "I'm an expert bus explorer now." He gave Robby an exaggerated wink.

Ty climbed over the rope and then up the stairs.

Robby watched the open windows and saw Ty walk down the aisle as if he were inspecting the bus for a sleeping child. He pointed at the only closed window along the right-hand side of the bus.

"This one?" Ty asked from inside.

Robby and Michelle both nodded.

"Yeah," Ty said, then shook his head. "There's no one on this bus. But it feels like the air conditioning is on."

Robby shuddered as if he, too, could feel the cold. As Ty descended the stairs and carefully navigated the ropes again, Robby watched the bus, almost afraid to blink in case he missed something.

"Kind of weird. I don't get it," Ty said. "Maybe you two should take a look."

Robby glanced at Michelle, who shook her head.

"Come on," Robby insisted. "We'll take a quick look and then we'll get out of here."

"Promise?" Michelle asked.

"Yes," Robby said. "I promise."

He hoped the lady at the front desk wasn't waiting to bust them for breaking the rules. After checking that the coast was clear, all three of them cautiously stepped over the blue rope. Robby slowly climbed the steps. The bus groaned a bit as they all clustered near the driver's seat.

Robby glanced down the aisle, expecting to see someone pop up and say *Gotcha! It's all just a prank, guys!*

No one did.

"Well, let's get this over with," Michelle said. "You go first Ty."

Robby followed his cousins down the aisle. With every careful step, the inside of the bus got chillier. He then felt an even cooler breeze brush past his cheek. *How could there be wind inside the bus? It's indoors and not moving!*

"It was this one," Ty whispered and pointed. It was the only closed window on the bus.

"Okay," Michelle whispered. "Found the closed window. Good work team. I think we're all set here."

And just like that, the window dropped open again.

Ty jumped back, knocking Michelle over, who fell down on top of Robby.

"Get off me!" Robby shouted.

"We have to get out of here!" Michelle cried.

"Get up, get up," Ty ordered.

Ty grabbed Michelle's hand and tugged her to her feet. She, in turn, snatched Robby up and pulled him to a standing position. Without having to be told again, all three of them bolted off the bus.

They scrambled down the stairs, nearly tripping over the rope in their desperate attempt to get away from the bus. Once he felt like he was at a safe distance, Robby turned and looked back at the window. It was still wide open, like the ones next to it. It was as if it had never been closed at all.

"What is going on here?" Robby wondered aloud. A chill ran along his scalp as if an icy finger was trying to get his attention. "How is that window closing and opening on its own?"

"The bus does that sometimes," the old lady from the front desk said, startling all of them.

She had walked through the door in the corner of the room. Her right hand gripped the rubber handle of a metal cane. Amazingly, she didn't seem upset by any of the noise and excitement the three of them had generated.

"That happens sometimes?" Michelle asked incredulously, hugging herself as if to keep warm and protected. "And you still work here?!"

The lady laughed. "Yes. And we've never figured out why that particular window does that."

Robby watched as the woman approached them. She looked at the bus and smiled. Seeing her calm and collected made him feel a little less frightened too.

All four of them stared at the bus for a moment as if they expected the window to close again.

The old woman broke the silence. "Some people have theories about what's happening here at the Hibbing Bus Museum."

"Like what?" Ty asked. "What do they say?"

"You haven't heard?" the lady asked, motioning with her cane around the garage. "This place is haunted."

CHAPTER 4

OUT-OF-TOWN INVESTIGATORS

The three cousins stared at one another with stunned expressions on their faces.

"This old place, haunted?" Ty asked.

The old woman shrugged and laughed a little. Robby thought it sounded like a cackle.

"At least that's what some people say. The museum hires a cleaning crew that comes once a week," she explained. "They tidy the place up in the middle of the night when it's extra quiet."

Robby thought about having to vacuum the floors and empty garbage cans with all of the silent, creepy mannequins around. He'd been startled when he turned around and saw one. Though he liked a good scare from time to time, Robby didn't think he'd like seeing the pale, frozen expressions of the dummies in the dead of night.

"So, what happens while they're cleaning?" Michelle asked. "The dummies come alive?"

"No, no," the woman said, with another cackle. "Nothing like that. They've claimed to see a little girl that appears and then disappears."

"No way," Ty whispered. "Like a ghost?"

Robby looked over his shoulder just then, feeling like he was being watched. He stared down the narrow path between two of the buses but didn't see anyone or anything. It felt like there were eyes everywhere, but he couldn't find a face. *Are there ghosts watching me from inside one of these buses?* Robby shuddered at the thought.

"Have you ever seen her?" Robby asked. "The little girl?"

The woman shook her head. "I haven't. But the buses make noise from time to time. They're old and creaky though, so I don't put too much stock into it." She paused, then added, "Word has spread that our museum is haunted. We even had a few ghost teams come in to try and capture something. It's been good for business."

Maybe not that good, Robby thought. *We're the only ones here.*

"Wait," Michelle said. "People are trying to catch the ghosts? That sounds like it wouldn't turn out well."

"No," Robby said. "They were probably trying to catch images of ghosts on camera or grab some EVPs."

Michelle turned and looked at Robby like *he* might be a ghost.

"EVPs are electronic voice phenomena," Robby explained. "It's where they try and get a voice recording of a ghost. Kind of spooky when they actually pick up something."

Michelle raised her eyebrows and looked at Ty, clearly amused at this new information about their cousin.

"Don't you ever watch those ghost shows?" Robby asked.

"No," Michelle replied. "Should I?"

Robby glanced around again, hoping to catch a glimpse of something.

"Yeah, I don't know. They're pretty cool," he admitted. "My dad and I watch them sometimes. I think a lot of the stuff in the shows are fake, but when they get something they can't explain, it's kind of fascinating."

Michelle shook her head. "Ty," she said, "did you have any idea that Robby was such a ghost dork?"

Ty didn't seem like he was in the mood to joke around anymore. He looked at Robby and shook his head.

"Any idea why this place might be haunted?" Robby asked the woman. "Did someone die in here or something?"

"Okay," Ty said, seeming more fidgety than usual. "We really should go."

Everyone else ignored him as the woman answered Robby's question.

"No one died inside the building that I'm aware of," she said quietly. She looked at the floor as if trying to look back through time. "But some of the ghost people who have come through here seem to think we're in a great location for paranormal activity."

At first, Robby wasn't sure what she meant, then it clicked.

"The cemetery," he whispered. "This museum is pretty much next door."

The woman nodded. "Bingo. They thought that maybe some of the lost souls from the graveyard wandered over here."

"Sure," Michelle said sarcastically. "I'm sure they just love looking at ancient bus junk."

Robby elbowed his cousin in her side to get her to stop. He was pretty sure it wasn't going to work.

The woman was about to respond when the telephone rang in the distance.

"Excuse me a moment, won't you?" she said. Before anyone could reply, the old woman shuffled through the exit Ty seemed eager to get to.

When the woman was gone and out of earshot, Ty spoke up. "Dead people from the graveyard? A creepy ghost girl? Lost spirits?"

Robby nodded excitedly, energized by this new information. "Yes," he said. "You know what I'm thinking?"

Michelle crossed her arms. "You promised me we'd leave."

"I know, and we will," Robby said. "Eventually."

"Didn't you say this place was boring?" Ty asked.

"Michelle probably did," Robby said. "She thinks everything is boring."

"Watch it," she snapped.

Robby grabbed his smartphone from his pocket and held it up like he was holding some new, revolutionary tool they'd never seen before.

"Let's try to capture something," Robby said. "On video! You know, unless you guys are too scared."

"The only thing I'm scared of is looking like an idiot," Michelle said, straightening her chin defiantly. "I'm in."

"But you think this museum is—" Ty began.

Michelle clapped him on the shoulder. "Yeah. Well? It just got a whole lot more interesting."

Climbing back aboard the bus, the three of them found seats near the window that decided to open and close on its own. Robby sat with his back to it, facing his cousins who sat across the aisle. Michelle looked nervous and Ty seemed like he wanted to be anywhere but on the bus.

"So how does this work?" Michelle asked. She drummed her fingernails on the top of the seat back.

"I think I just hit record and . . ."

"I know how the app works, Slobby," Michelle snapped. "This whole goofy talking-to-ghosts ritual. How does *that* work?"

Robby laughed. He hadn't been called "Slobby" since he was eight years old.

Leave it to Michelle to bring out a classic!

"We just record and ask questions," Robby said. "That's how the pros do it. I mean, they have much fancier equipment, but this might work."

Michelle took a deep breath and exhaled nice and loud. It seemed like her way of saying she was merely putting up with Robby's spooky experiment. Ty rubbed his hands together as if trying to keep warm. It was chilly in the bus, which was odd considering it wasn't running and was stuck inside a muggy museum on Fourth of July weekend.

"Okay," Robby said once everyone seemed settled. "Let's start."

He pressed the red RECORD button on his phone. Since he didn't know where to point it, he panned very slowly back and forth. Every time he passed Michelle and Ty, she raised her eyebrows. Ty just looked toward the exit as if ready to leave at any moment.

A few minutes passed and no one said a word.

"Aren't you supposed to ask questions?" Ty asked.

"Yeah," Robby replied. "I suppose."

He cleared his throat.

"Is there anyone here with us today?"

Michelle looked at her two cousins. Robby could tell that she was *dying* to make a joke but held off. A long moment of silence followed. He couldn't hear anything in the way of a response.

"We heard that sometimes there's a little girl who

shows up here at the museum," Robby said. He looked up at the bus's ceiling as if something might appear there.

"Do you see anything on your phone, Robby?" Ty whispered.

Robby shook his head. He kept quiet for a moment or two then asked another question.

"What is your name?"

As the words left his mouth, Robby felt like the bus got another few degrees colder. It reminded him of the quick blast of cold air he felt when someone opened the front door during a Minnesota winter. He shivered and saw that both Michelle and Ty felt it too.

"It just got colder in here," Michelle whispered.

Robby scanned the bus, looking to see if his video recorder might be catching something. There didn't seem to be anything but the animated faces of his cousins.

"We just want to talk to you," Robby said. "We're not here to harm you or make you leave."

Of all the paranormal shows Robby watched, the ones where the investigators were respectful to the spirits and ghosts were his favorite. There were others where the paranormal "pros" shouted and dared the dead to do something to prove they were real. Robby thought shows where they provoked ghosts were fake and pretty uninteresting overall.

"Anything yet?" Michelle asked quietly. She was visibly shivering in the bus but seemed willing to stick it out just to prove she wasn't afraid. Robby wasn't sure Michelle was afraid of anything.

"No," Robby whispered. "I just see you two looking cold and miserable."

Robby peered out the window. He was surprised the front desk lady hadn't come back. He wondered how she'd feel about them holding an impromptu séance inside the museum.

One last question before we get out of here.

"We want to know more about you," Robby said. "Will you talk to us?"

He let the silence hang in the aisle for a bit as he felt colder and colder with every passing moment.

"Creepy," Ty whispered.

"What?" Robby said. "Did you see something?"

"No," Ty insisted. "You're creepy."

And with that, Robby stopped recording. It was time to give it a rest, and besides feeling literally chilled to the bone, they didn't get anything.

"We done?" Michelle asked. She stood up and rubbed her hands up and down her arms to warm up.

"Yeah," Robby said. "We're not going to get anything here. On most of those shows the investigators are at a haunted place for like a week. And they chop all the boring stuff out and just show you the weird things they might have picked up."

The three of them climbed off the bus and walked past the waiting throng of mannequins gathered outside. As soon as they were fifty feet from the bus, Robby felt himself warm up again. It was like the bus was a constant source of cold.

"So? What do you think?" Michelle asked as they walked out into the main area and toward the exit. "This place haunted or what?"

They walked through the area where the uniforms and the single mannequin in the dark suit was standing near the display cases.

"I don't know," Robby admitted. "The temperature makes me wonder if there's something hanging around. Some ghost experts think that cold spots mean there's something paranormal there."

"Really?" Michelle asked. "They'd lose their mind in South Dakota or here in the winter. It's cold everywhere."

"Very funny," Robby said. "But it shouldn't have been that cold in the bus. Not in July."

"Well, who knows," Michelle said. "Could be a draft or maybe there was an air conditioner vent right below the bus. What do you think Ty?"

They turned to see Ty standing near the mini theater that was playing the history of the bus company. Standing near the wall was their old mascot, Tooty the cartoon bus.

"I think Tooty moved," Ty said in a raised whisper. "From the bus garage all the way over here."

Robby looked at the little replica. It was about the size of a cooler, but boxier and made to look like a bus

with eyes and a smiling, happy mouth. He still held the HEY KIDS! I'M TOOTY! sign.

Robby touched the mascot and gave it a slight push. He was surprised by how heavy it was.

"Maybe the old lady moved it," Michelle offered.

Ty wasn't convinced. "And Tooty's eyes," he whispered. "I think they moved too."

CHAPTER 5

CONTACT

"That's crazy," Robby said, studying Tooty carefully. "You sure his eyes weren't like that already?"

Ty shook his head and looked as pale as a, well, ghost.

"Tooty was looking straight ahead," Ty whispered. "Now he's looking off to the side."

Robby looked at the eyes again. He tried to remember what the little bus looked like from when they first got there.

"Maybe it's battery powered and moves from time to time," Robby suggested.

"Or there's a ghost living inside Tooty," Michelle suggested, making ghost noises and waving her hands like she was one.

"Don't even say that," Ty said, holding his sights on Tooty the whole time. "And don't be ridiculous."

Robby glanced around the museum to see if there was anything else out of place. Nothing seemed disturbed. The eyes didn't puzzle Robby, but what did was that the little bus mascot had moved from the garage to the main exhibit area.

"I don't know about the eyes," Robby said finally. "But it is a little weird that ol' Tooty is in here now."

"Really?" Michelle asked. "You don't think someone else who works here maybe moved that goofy little bus? And maybe when he or she set it down, the eyes moved a little bit?"

Robby shrugged. He supposed it was possible.

Is there someone else besides the front desk lady here at the museum?

"Maybe it's the little girl," Ty whispered. "Maybe she's playing with the bus."

"I doubt it," Robby said. "Guys, maybe we've got it in our heads that the place is haunted because the lady said it is. Now we're thinking that anything that's happening is weird because of some ghosts or spirits in this place."

"Then explain the window," Ty said.

He's got me there, Robby thought.

Considering he was going to likely have to share a tent with Ty, Robby realized he needed to do whatever he could to keep him from getting too scared and worked up. The last thing he needed was for Ty to have nightmares and wake him up in the middle of the night. He knew it would be hard enough to sleep in the tent as it was.

"Look, this place is plenty creepy, but I don't think it's haunted," Robby said. "I didn't see anything on the videos I recorded. And I've seen plenty of ghost shows to know that there's nothing to be scared of here."

C'mon, Ty. Believe me, even if I don't believe it myself.

"I don't know," Ty said. "Even the lady said it's haunted."

"Okay," Robby said. "So, someone moved this little bus. It's probably a guy who works behind the scenes or something. And the thing with the window? It could be anything. Maybe the wind from an air vent?"

Ty crossed his arms and raised one of his eyebrows. He wasn't buying it.

"Nice try," Michelle whispered.

"Fine," Robby said. "So, maybe not, but it's not something we need to worry about. Let's just head back to Uncle Stewart's and forget all about this place, okay?"

"Yeah," Ty said. "Good idea."

As they walked toward the exit, Robby watched Ty look back over his shoulder at the little goofy bus. He clearly wasn't going to let it go.

They walked outside and found their borrowed bikes waiting for them. *I'd rather be stuck talking to Aunt Julie and her garbage-pail breath than be in this place one second longer*, Robby thought.

"Race ya to the stop sign," he called to his cousins, and shoved off.

———————

The three of them got back to the cabin without any problems, mostly because Robby didn't even think about touching his bike's self-destruct stick shift. They spent the next few hours catching up with the family and telling them about their museum adventure.

Their older cousin Lisa seemed fascinated by what they found.

"A haunted bus museum?" she asked. "Like ghost buses?"

"No," Ty said. "Ghosts in the buses."

"She's messing with you," Robby whispered. "She totally doesn't believe you."

They got similar reactions from other members of the Warner family. They all made jokes about friendly cartoon ghosts and pretended to see spirits over their shoulders.

"Pro tip," Michelle said as she threw her paper plate

and a few uneaten pieces of cheese into the garbage. "Let's not talk about the ghost stuff with these guys anymore. We sound like morons and I hate being the butt of their jokes."

"Good call," Robby said.

"Yeah," Ty agreed.

As it grew dark, some of the family started to set up tents across Uncle Stewart's property. There were so many tents that instead of looking like private property, it looked like a campground.

Their cousin Jim came by and cracked open a soda. He drank the whole thing without stopping for a breath, and then belched. He crushed the can and tossed it into the plastic barrel marked RECYCLING.

"Impressive," Michelle said.

"Thanks, Shell-Bell," he said.

Michelle rolled her eyes.

Jim continued, unfazed. "We got the tents all set up. You and Jenny are over there."

Jim pointed to a four-person tent along the edge of the property. He then pointed to a smaller tent near the one Michelle was going to sleep in.

"Robby," Jim said. "You and the little guy are going to be in that one."

Ty stood up from the picnic table.

"That's tiny," he protested.

"Little guy, little tent," Jim said. "That's how it works, buddy."

Perfect. We're going to be packed in that little tent like a couple of sardines.

He only hoped Ty didn't end up having bad dreams.

———

Later that night, he and Ty unzipped the flaps of the tent and climbed in to find their sleeping bags waiting for them. They were both worn out from the day of traveling, biking, and enduring a big family function.

As Robby zipped the tent closed, he noticed Ty had already flopped down face-first onto his sleeping bag. He didn't seem to be in a hurry to climb inside.

"Think you'll be able to sleep okay?" Robby asked.

As an answer, he heard soft snoring coming from his cousin.

"So, that's a yes," Robby whispered, feeling relieved.

He opened his sleeping bag as quietly as possible and slipped in. The inner fabric was warm and cozy but he only had one small pillow to work with. He was used to having three on his bed back home.

Robby lay on his back and looked up at the dark ceiling of their tent. Some of his cousins were still awake playing cards on the deck. He could hear them laughing and talking. The loudest noise, though, came from the chorus of chirping crickets. It sounded like there were a billion of them.

Getting to sleep wasn't going to be easy.

Robby turned to his side, hoping to block one of his ears and halve the noise from outside. It didn't seem to help. Realizing he was in for a long night, he picked up his smartphone, opened the flashlight app, and found his earbuds tucked into his backpack.

Squinting from the phone's bright light, he turned it to see that Ty hadn't moved from his original position. The kid was still face down and snoring like nothing was going to wake him up.

"Lucky," Robby whispered.

He played a few games on his phone until he was tired of them, then tried to watch an online video. The playback was choppy as the internet connection near Viridian Lake was less than reliable.

It was then that he thought about the video he made on the bus with Michelle and Ty.

Robby navigated to the video app on his phone and found the file. He tapped PLAY and watched as his cousins' faces appeared inside the old bus. By the expressions on their faces, they looked like they were miserable. Mostly likely because it was cold, and Michelle thought the whole thing was absurd.

He heard himself ask the first question: *"Is there anyone here with us today?"* Robby looked at the screen, hoping to see if the phone captured something he missed while recording.

Nothing.

Then, *"We heard that sometimes there's a little girl who shows up here at the museum."*

Robby sighed. He didn't like the sound of his voice and wondered why a recording of it sounded so much different than from when he spoke normally. He intently watched the video as his recording moved back and forth slowly from the front to the back of the bus.

Still nothing.

"What is your name?" Robby asked on the video.

He didn't see anything on the video, so he lifted his finger to turn it off. Just then, Robby heard something.

It was faint and almost inaudible.

"Whoa," Robby whispered. He tapped the PAUSE button and scrolled back a few seconds. He dragged the volume control slider up to its maximum.

"What is your name?" he heard himself ask again.

"John," a voice said in a hoarse whisper.

"You have to be kidding me!" Robby shouted, completely forgetting his younger cousin was sleeping about a foot away from him.

Ty stirred in his sleep and mumbled something Robby couldn't understand. It was hard for Robby to hear over the adrenaline ringing in his ears and the thunder-like beating of his heart. He couldn't believe it. They had wanted to capture an image of a ghost on camera. Instead, he had audio.

"John," Robby whispered. "It's not a little girl at all."

He paused the video for a moment to catch his breath. The image froze on Ty's face. He was looking around as if he was worried and terrified to even be in the bus. When he felt like he was ready, Robby tapped PLAY again.

"We just want to talk to you," Robby heard himself say in the recording. *"We're not here to harm you or make you leave."*

He strained to hear if there was a response from John. Silence. Robby took a deep breath. He hoped that wasn't it.

"We want to know more about you," Robby said on the video. *"Will you talk to us?"*

"Yes," came John's reply.

Robby let out his breath in a rush and let the video play. He realized that was the last question he asked the ghost. The final thing he heard on the recording was Ty telling him that he thought Robby was creepy. After that, he'd stopped recording.

"No!" Robby whispered.

A ghost named John wanted to talk to us and we walked away, Robby thought.

He unzipped his sleeping bag. He knew what he had to do.

CHAPTER 6

VOICE IN THE DARK

Robby walked across the long grass to the medium-sized tent nearby. It was dark inside, which meant Michelle was probably sleeping. He raised his hand to knock, but realized it wasn't possible to knock on a tent's door flaps.

"Michelle," Robby whispered softly, but hopefully loud enough for her to hear.

There was no answer.

"*Pssst*," Robby hissed. "Michelle. Wake up."

He looked at his phone and saw what time it was. Almost 11:00 p.m. It was late, but he didn't think it could wait until morning. Besides, morning was technically only an hour away, anyway.

"Michelle!"

Still no answer.

Desperate for his cousin to hear the video, he unzipped the tent flap and climbed in. Using the light from his phone, he found Michelle fast asleep. He did his best to be quiet and not wake his older cousin Jenny who was sleeping on the other side of the tent.

"Hey," Robby said, shaking Michelle's shoulder. "Wake up."

Michelle stirred and groaned.

"Still tired," she murmured.

"I got something," Robby said, ignoring what she said. "Get up, would you?"

"Quiet time," Michelle whispered, still mostly asleep.

Robby shook her again.

"Okay, creepy," Michelle said, after releasing a deep sigh. It sounded like she was finally rousted from sleep. "I'm seriously going to punch you in the mouth. What are you doing? And why are you in here?"

"I got something on my phone," Robby said.

"We all do, dummy," Michelle said, sitting up. "Songs, apps, photos . . ."

"No, no," Robby said. Even half awake his cousin was a smart aleck. "I captured a ghost voice on here."

"An EBP?" she asked, rubbing her eyes.

"EVP," Robby said, correcting her.

"Whatever," Michelle said and waved her hands. "Wait. Are you serious?"

Robby grabbed his earbuds and plugged them into Michelle's ears.

"Oh gross," she said. "Did you wipe these off first? I don't want your earwax."

Robby ignored her and played the first bit. He watched his cousin's face in the light from his phone. She looked bored and disinterested and then suddenly her eyes widened, and she gave him a stunned look.

Michelle ripped the earbuds from her ears.

"Shut up!" she shouted.

"Will *you* two shut up?" their cousin Jenny called from the other side of the four-person tent. "Some of us are trying really hard to sleep!"

Michelle lowered her voice to a whisper.

"Did you do something to this recording?" she asked. "Like add that voice or something?"

"No," Robby said, his face solemn. "I swear on a Nolan Ryan autographed baseball card that I didn't."

"Wow. That was specific. Okay, then let me hear more," Michelle insisted, plugging the earbuds back into her ears.

Robby rewound the recording so it started playing again at the beginning. After hearing the whole thing again, she shook her head as she took out the earbuds.

"He wanted to talk to us," Michelle said, "and we just walked away."

"I know," Robby said. "But I guess I know what we're doing tomorrow."

"They open at 9:00 a.m.," Michelle said through a mouthful of milk and Chocolate Action Pops. She looked at her phone while eating breakfast the next morning.

"Perfect," Robby replied and took a swig of his orange juice.

It was just after 8:00 a.m. Robby was surprised either of them were able to fall asleep after his paranormal discovery. He figured if they left right after breakfast, they'd be able to get to the museum just before it opened. If they were lucky, they'd be the only ones there, besides the lady at the front desk.

"Think we can sneak away before Ty notices?" Michelle asked, looking around at the other members of the Warner clan who were already up.

The back screen door of the cabin squeaked open and in walked their youngest cousin. Ty's hair was sticking up in wild tufts and he looked completely exhausted. He saw Michelle and Robby and raised a hand in a half-awake wave.

"Nope," Robby whispered to Michelle.

Seeing there was no way around it, Robby brought Ty up to speed. Though he warned his cousin that the voice was going to sound creepy and could give him nightmares, Ty insisted on hearing it. When he was done his face looked like he'd just hopped out of the front seat of a roller coaster.

"No way," he whispered.

"We're going back to the museum," Robby said. "We need to see if we can talk to John again. I don't want you to feel like—"

"I'm coming too," Ty interrupted.

"Tooty is going to be there," Michelle teased.

"I don't care," Ty said. "I'd rather be creeped out and try to talk to some ghost than be stuck here all day."

"Okay, then," Robby nodded. "Eat up, kid. We leave in five minutes."

———

The three of them rolled their classic bikes into the parking lot of the Hibbing Bus Museum just as the lady from the front desk was unlocking the door. She turned to watch them ride up to the sidewalk and smiled, squinting in the morning sun.

"Well, look who's back," she said and cackled out a laugh. "Back to see the rest of the museum?"

"There's more?" Ty asked.

Robby wanted to elbow him in the ribs. He didn't exactly want the lady to know they were planning on sitting inside the bus again to try and make contact with the ghost.

"Oh my, yes," she said. "You kids missed all of the buses we have parked outside. There's plenty more to see."

I'm sure, Robby thought. *But the stuff we want to see isn't so easy to see.*

They parked their rides under the museum's front awning and followed the woman in. As she set her stuff down and got behind the desk, Robby produced three dollar bills.

"It's on me," Robby said.

"Mr. Moneybags," Michelle said. "Can you get me a T-shirt, too?"

"Probably not," Robby replied before leading them into the museum.

The three of them walked past the familiar displays and almost immediately, Ty breathed a sigh of relief. He took a few cautious steps near Tooty, who was still where they'd seen him last. The little bus didn't seem any different than when they'd left him.

"It's still kind of creepy," Ty mumbled.

"Remember," Robby reminded his cousin. "We're not going to run off all scared. We want to try and talk to John. You can't beg us to leave or anything."

"I won't," Ty said. "Really, I won't."

The three of them headed past the uniformed mannequin and through the door that led to the indoor bus garage. They weaved between a few buses until they found the one with the dummies congregating in front of it.

"All right," Robby said, and then took a deep breath. "You guys ready?"

"Yeah," Michelle said, looking at Ty. "At least I am."

"I'm ready, guys," Ty insisted. "Let's do this."

They snuck past the ropes, climbed the stairs, and made their way to the same seats they were in last time. Robby pulled out his earbuds, plugged them into his phone, and popped them into his ears. Without waiting any longer, he started recording.

"We're back," Robby said. "John? If you're here with us, will you talk with us again?"

They all remained silent, as if waiting for a response. Again, as the day before, they couldn't hear anything.

"I'm sorry we left so soon after you talked with us," Robby said apologetically. "I couldn't hear you before. I'm hoping you weren't too upset."

Ty shifted in his seat and glanced over his shoulder.

"You have to quit doing that," Michelle whispered to her younger cousin. "You're freaking me out."

"Sorry," Ty said. "I keep thinking I saw something."

A familiar cold settled inside the bus as if coming from nowhere. Robby watched as the skin on his arms became bumpy. Michelle pulled the sleeves of her sweatshirt down. Knowing it was going to be cold, she'd planned ahead.

"Will you talk with us, John?" Robby asked.

He waited long enough for an answer, then stopped the recording.

"Wait," Ty asked. "What're you doing?"

"I can only hear him when I play it back," Robby explained and quickly played the short clip back.

He strained to listen. After asking the second time if they could talk to him, Robby heard a raspy *"Yes."*

"John's here," Robby announced. He hit PLAY to record another video. "He wants to talk to us."

Michelle hugged herself and nodded. Ty leaned across the aisle as if to get closer to Robby.

"Can you tell us why you're here, John?" Robby asked. "Were you a bus driver?"

Michelle gave him a strange look.

"What?" Robby said. "He could be, right? They say that sometimes ghosts are attached to things they used a lot in the real world. Like if you were a ghost, maybe you'd haunt a cheese factory."

Ty laughed.

"Oh I, want to hit you so bad right now," Michelle said.

Another wave of cold washed over them and Robby could feel that John's spirit was with them. As an afterthought, he spoke again.

"I'm sorry," Robby said. "I didn't tell you who we are. I'm Robby Warner from Oakdale, Minnesota. I'll let these two introduce themselves."

"I'm Tyrone Hernandez," Ty said. "I live in New Ulm, Minnesota. It's like five hours away from here. It was a really long drive."

They both turned to Michelle.

"Are you serious?" she asked. When both Robby and Ty nodded, she played along. "Fine. I'm Michelle Berger. I'm from Sioux Falls, South Dakota."

Robby smiled to show Michelle he was glad she'd done that.

"We're cousins," Robby explained. "We're in town for the Warner family reunion."

"I bet he doesn't care," Michelle said. "Listen back."

Robby stopped the recording and played back what he'd asked the ghost.

"Can you tell us why you're here, John?" Robby heard himself ask. The answer came back almost immediately: *"Helen."*

"Were you a bus driver?" John's response was simple. *"No."*

Robby listened to the rest of the recording and couldn't hear anything else.

"What did you hear?" Michelle demanded. "Your face did a thing before."

"He's here because of Helen," Robby said. "Here, listen."

He took out his earbuds and passed them to Michelle. She gave one of the earpieces to Ty and they each plugged one in. Robby played the clip for them and watched as they both took in what John had said.

"Helen," Michelle said when the video was done.

"That's really what he said, right?" Robby wanted to make sure he wasn't just hearing things. Too many times on the paranormal shows he watched, what they thought they heard didn't sound the same to Robby.

"Yeah," Ty said. "But that leaves us with a big question."

Robby and Michelle turned to their younger cousin.

"Who's Helen?" Ty whispered.

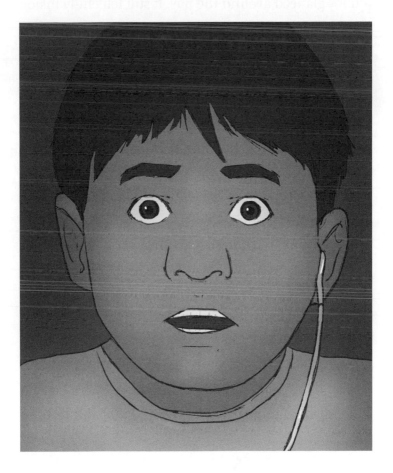

CHAPTER 7

GRAVE NEIGHBORS

Robby glanced around the bus. It still felt chilly inside the big metal corridor, but not as cold as it had been moments before. Ty had brought up a great question and it didn't seem like any of them had answers.

"We should ask John," Robby said, quickly getting his video up ready to record.

"This is getting spookier by the second," Michelle whispered.

Robby let his thumb hover over the red RECORD button on his phone's screen.

"You think we should stop?" he asked.

Michelle shook her head no. So did Ty.

"No," Ty said. "We have to figure this out."

"Good," Robby said. "I think so too."

He hit RECORD and took a deep breath as if to calm himself down.

"Hi John," Robby said. "It's us again. We're hoping you still want to talk to us. You said that you're here at the museum because of Helen. Can you tell us who Helen is?"

Robby paused to give the ghost some time to respond. As he did, what felt like a cold draft passed through his body. It made him shiver for a moment, then the feeling was gone. He looked at his cousins to see if they'd experienced the same thing. Neither of them seemed disturbed by the temperature changes in the bus.

"I feel like it's getting warmer in here," Michelle said suddenly.

"Might be because you're wearing a sweatshirt," Robby said.

Michelle shrugged.

"I'll listen to it," Robby said and stopped recording. "I'm not sure what to ask him until we know who Helen is and why she's what's keeping him here."

He pulled up the video file and listened to himself asking the question and the silence that followed. After a few moments, he heard Michelle say it was getting warmer in the bus. There was nothing following his question.

"What'd he say?" Ty asked.

"Hold on," Robby said. "I'm going to listen again."

He pressed the volume control until it was at MAX, then replayed the video. He winced as his voice came through extra loud and listened into the quiet after his question. It sounded like he could hear the oxygen moving through the air and his cousins' breathing, but that was it.

No voice.

"Nothing," Robby said and stopped. "He didn't say anything."

"Well, try again," Michelle said. "I mean, maybe we didn't give him enough time."

Robby nodded. He made five more attempts to contact John and each and every time he came back with nothing. By the time he was done listening to the last video, the inside of the bus was no longer cool at all. The humidity from the July heat began to creep into the museum.

"I hate to say it, guys," Robby said. "But I think John is gone."

"Why wouldn't he answer?" Michelle asked. "It doesn't make sense."

Robby shrugged. "On those shows I watch, they say it takes a lot of energy for spirits to do anything, including talk. Maybe he didn't have enough energy to do much more than answer a few questions."

Ty smiled. "You sure know a lot about this stuff."

"I don't know about that," Robby admitted. "Just what I've seen on TV or whatever."

Michelle stood up. "So we're never going to figure out who this Helen is, then? I mean, we're only here another day. We can't keep coming back and asking a couple questions at a time."

Robby hadn't thought of that. After tomorrow night's fireworks, they were all headed back home in the morning. He doubted the museum was even open on the Fourth of July. If they couldn't figure out why John was there soon, he didn't think they ever would.

"Who could Helen be?" Ty asked. "Do you think it's the lady at the front desk?"

"Could be," Robby said. "Maybe she knows something about him."

"Let's go, then," Michelle said. "I'm getting kind of sick of sitting on a bus that isn't going anywhere."

They climbed back out of the bus and took the quickest path to the front desk area where the lady was helping a family of four with their admission fees. They boy and girl were much younger, and Robby couldn't help but wonder if they were going to be a little frightened by the mannequins.

Once the coast was clear, they approached the front desk.

"Well, that was pretty quick," the lady said. "Did you already get outside and see those other buses?"

"Not exactly," Robby said. "But I wanted to ask you a question."

The lady smiled as if prepared to answer any question Robby might have about Hibbing Bus Lines and its storied history.

"Can we ask what your name is?" Robby asked. He clenched his teeth in anticipation of her answer. Maybe if her name was Helen, she could explain who John was and they could have the whole mystery solved in a matter of minutes.

"It's Martha," the woman replied. "Why?"

"So your middle name isn't Helen or something?" Michelle asked, stepping in front of Robby.

"Uh, no," Martha replied. "It's Louise."

"Well, that stinks," Michelle muttered, and turned to her cousins. "So much for that idea."

"I beg your pardon?" Martha asked. The woman looked like she'd been slapped across the face.

Robby decided he'd better step in.

"No, no," Robby explained. "It's not that your name stinks. It's really a nice couple of names. It's just that . . ."

Great, now I've got to come out with it.

"We were able to talk to the ghost in the bus," he said quickly. "He said his name is John and he's here because of Helen. We tried to get him to tell us who Helen is, but he hasn't said anything else."

"He probably got tired," Ty said quickly.

Martha smiled at Ty in a way a grandmother does when her grandchild says something cute.

"Do you have any idea who Helen could be?" Robby asked. He couldn't help but feel like they were officially bugging the lady, but he didn't know what else to do.

"I'm sorry," Martha admitted. "I don't know anybody named Helen and there hasn't been anyone with that name working here that I know of."

Dead end, Robby thought. *Yet again.*

"Maybe you could talk to some of the other ghost teams that have been here," Martha suggested. "But from what I've heard, they haven't found too much either. They've seen some shadows and heard some voices, but I don't think they're any closer to figuring out what's happening here."

"Okay," Robby said. He was starting to feel defeated. "Thanks for your help."

Martha looked at the three of them with something that resembled pity.

"If it makes you feel any better you three have gotten a lot further in a short amount of time than any of the other people who—"

Just then, a door leading to the outside on their immediate left flew open, casting bright July sunlight into the museum. As all four of them looked, a faint shadowy figure stepped through it.

"Did you see that?" Ty gasped, his eyes wide with horror. He put his hands to the side of his head as if to keep it from flying off his neck in complete shock.

"No way," Michelle whispered. "No way, no way, no way."

Robby was speechless. A full-bodied something walked right out of the museum.

"Oh, that door," Martha groaned. "I wanted Bill to fix the latch on it, but he just hasn't been able to."

"Wait," Robby said, trying to talk though his heart was beating like a drum. "Didn't you see that?"

"That old door flying open?" Martha asked. "I sure did. The wind catches it just right and it flies open on its own. It's the darndest thing and we've had to disconnect the emergency doo-dads from the door so that the alarm doesn't go off."

"No, no," Ty said. "A ghost just walked through that doorway! While we were standing here!"

Martha pulled a pair of glasses from a worn light-brown leather case. She placed them on the bridge of her nose and squinted. After a moment, she shook her head.

"I don't see anything," she said finally. "Just sunlight and trees."

Robby couldn't take his eyes off the door. He noticed that the leaves on the trees across the parking lot were almost completely still. There wasn't any wind and if there was, it wasn't enough to open a solid metal door.

Martha hadn't seen the spirit.

"What if it was John?" Michelle whispered, leaning in close to Robby. "Maybe he's had it with this museum and is going to find a new place to haunt."

Robby exhaled and glanced at his cousin. She in turn shrugged and nodded toward the door.

"Maybe we should check it out," she said.

Robby turned to Martha. "We're going to have a look if that's all right?"

"Of course," Martha said. "And would you be a dear and close it behind you?"

The three of them walked away from the front desk and headed for the open door. As Robby got close, he felt an odd sensation. The air was warm and humid, but there was an undercurrent of cold as his left arm passed near the open door. It almost felt like someone was holding a frigid ice pop near his skin, while the rest of him felt much warmer.

"Do you feel that?" Robby asked.

"Yeah," Ty replied, but looked out toward the trees. "But where did he go?"

Michelle pointed. "I have an idea where."

They all stepped outside, and Robby pulled the door closed behind them. The door was cold to the touch. He heard it latch. Robby then pulled the handle and found the door was locked.

"Wind didn't do this," Robby said, hoping Martha wouldn't hear. "It was pushed open from the inside."

"By John?" Ty asked.

"I guess so," Robby replied.

"You guys," Michelle said, walking forward. "He totally went through here and into the graveyard."

Robby looked away from the door. Through the trees he saw the bright white headstones that dotted the large expanse of green grass. Some of the grave markers were just flat rectangles, while others were tall tombstones with fancier designs added to them.

"Let's take a look," Robby suggested and headed toward the trees that lined the museum property.

"Yeah, I don't love this idea," Ty said, but followed his cousins anyway.

They passed through the small wooded area that divided the museum from the cemetery. When they reached the cemetery, they stopped. Robby gazed across the horizon at all the graves. He'd never really been afraid of graveyards, but knowing they'd followed a ghost to one changed things a bit.

"Do you see him?" Michelle asked. "Because I sure don't."

Robby looked carefully, trying to see if the shadow he saw was anywhere to be found. He didn't know for sure that it was even John or if it had entered the cemetery. It just seemed to make sense.

Maybe he's going back to where he belongs.

"No," Robby said finally and sighed. "I don't see anything but graves. Lots and lots of graves."

"Do you think he's buried out there somewhere?" Ty asked. "And that's where he goes when it's time to rest?"

"Who knows?" Robby replied, before Michelle could make a joke out of it. "But maybe Martha was right. Maybe the ghosts in the museum are just wandering souls from the graveyard. And maybe John is done with the place now."

It didn't seem right to Robby, but he wasn't sure what else to think.

It still doesn't explain who Helen is. Maybe we're just not meant to know.

CHAPTER 8

SHADOW TALK

Robby and his cousins did their best to try and forget about John. They didn't want to think about the possibility that his shadowy ghost might have walked out of the museum and into the Hibbing Park Cemetery. They knew the museum was going to be closed for the Fourth of July, so they figured they'd gotten as far as they could.

After riding their vintage bikes back to the cabin, they all agreed to try and find something else to do to pass the time. They found a few old board games in Uncle Stewart's closet, but most of them were missing a handful of the game pieces they needed. Ty completely destroyed his cousins playing the ones that were intact. Michelle didn't like to lose, so after a few games she quit.

Later, Robby swatted more rocks into the green waters of Viridian Lake with a baseball bat, Michelle took a nap, and Ty played with their cousin Teddy's dog for a few hours.

Much later that night, Robby, Michelle, and Ty sat up inside Michelle's tent. Their cousin Jenny agreed to trade tents so that she could get some sleep for a change. It seemed like a fair trade. The three of them would share the four-person tent and Jenny could have the small one all to herself.

Win-win.

"I know we're not supposed to talk about it," Ty began. He cringed thinking one of them would belt him in the shoulder.

"Don't," Michelle said. "Don't do it, Ty."

"But I can't stop thinking about that shadow we saw," he finished. Ty squeezed his eyes shut, prepared for the blow. No one hit him.

"I've been doing my best to forget about it," Robby admitted. "But I can't. I keep telling myself that it was just that: a shadow. Only, I don't know. It was something."

"You guys suck," Michelle said. "And you had to bring it up at like eleven-something at night."

"Sorry," Ty said. "I'm just glad you're all in here with me."

"Really?" Michelle said with a sly smile. "Because I was just thinking about throwing you out."

"Seriously?" Ty asked, his eyes wide.

Michelle shrugged and then pushed Ty over, which Robby knew was her way of showing that she was just kidding. Ty tipped over and laughed, which was a good sign.

"I wish I would've had my video going," Robby said. "It would've been pretty slick to play it back and analyze it."

"I have to admit, I'm glad you didn't," Michelle said. "That way I can pretend we all just imagined it."

Robby tried to think back to what he and his cousins had seen. It all happened so fast. The door blasting open and the shadow that seemed to walk right through it.

"At least we'll have fireworks and stuff to distract us tomorrow night," Ty said.

"There you go," Michelle said. "Let's think about the pretty explosions and not some dead guy's spirit trying to talk to us."

"Not helping," Ty muttered.

The youngest cousin lay down on his unrolled sleeping bag and stared up at the tent's ceiling. Robby did the same, trying to make himself as comfortable as possible. There was a half-moon in the sky that cast shadows from a dead tree onto the tent.

"Didn't Martha say some of the investigators saw a little girl in the museum?" Ty asked.

"Yeah," Robby said. "But I thought we decided we were done talking about this."

"What if the little girl is Helen?" Ty proposed.

Every hair on Robby's arms and legs stood up at attention.

The kid might be a genius, Robby thought. *Are the two ghosts connected somehow? Is John looking for the little girl? Is it his daughter?*

"Okay," Michelle said. "I really wish you'd just stop talking, Ty. As it stands, I'm not going to be able to sleep tonight, let alone for the rest of my life."

Robby turned to see Michelle climb into her sleeping bag, which was laid out on an inflatable mattress. *If she isn't going to be able to fall asleep, at least she'll be comfortable staring into space until morning,* he thought, a bit jealously.

The three of them lay in silence, listening to the last few members of the Warner family talking and the steady chirping of Hibbing's finest insects. Somewhere in the distance, a dog barked.

After the rest of the family finally went to bed and Robby began to relax, he tried closing his eyes. It was then that it felt like the temperature in their shared tent dropped ten degrees. He opened his eyes and saw a shadow cast on the nylon ceiling of their tent.

It wasn't dead tree branch shadows anymore. It was in the shape of a person.

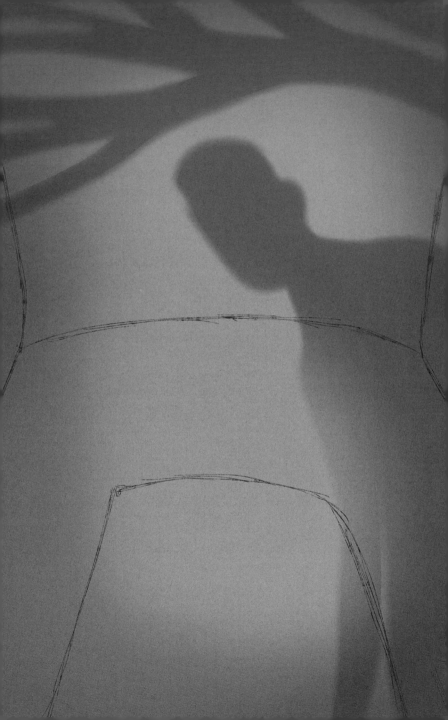

"Robby?!?" Michelle whispered. "Do you see that?"

Robby turned and could see her pale, moonlit face. A moment later, Ty sat up. His mouth gaped open and he looked like he was on the verge of screaming or crying or both. Before he could, Robby clapped a hand over Ty's mouth.

"John?" Robby asked. "Is that you?"

There was no answer. If it was one of his older cousins trying to scare them or screw around, he wanted to know. Somehow, he knew that it wasn't.

"Look out your window," Robby whispered to Michelle. "See if it's one of our knuckleheaded cousins."

Michelle hesitated as if she had no interest in looking out into the yard. She unzipped a little bit of the tent's window and peered through the gap. A second later, she zipped it back up, turned to Robby and shook her head. Her face looked blank with fear.

"What?"

"There's no one there," Michelle said quietly. "Absolutely no one."

Robby felt his pulse quicken and turned his attention to Ty who still looked like he wanted to scream, even with a hand over his mouth.

"Don't do it," Robby said.

"Mi mon't," Ty mumbled.

Robby released his little cousin from his grasp, then looked to the shadow. It was still standing there in the moonlight as if waiting or even worse . . .

Watching.

On his hands and knees, Robby fumbled around on the plastic tent floor until he felt his smartphone. He unlocked it, inserted his earbuds, and immediately brought up the video app. He pressed record and aimed it at the shadow. In the dim light, it was hard to make out the shadow's shape, but he could see it.

"John?" Robby asked. "Are you here with us?"

Almost immediately, Robby heard an answer.

"Yes."

"Whoa," Robby cried. He pulled his earbuds out and almost threw his phone across the tent.

"What?" Michelle whispered. She had climbed off her air mattress and was sitting as close as she could tolerate to Ty. "What happened?"

"I could hear him," Robby gasped. "Like without playing it back."

"Then why did you tear your earbuds out?" Ty asked.

"It freaked me out," Robby replied. He was finding it

hard to catch his breath. "I don't know why it's working like this."

His cousins alternated looking at Robby and glancing back at the looming shadow. The figure didn't seem to move or react in any way. It just stood as if watching them through the thin fabric of the tent. Robby hurriedly grabbed the earbuds and plugged them back into his ears.

"So that's him?" Michelle asked.

Robby nodded slowly. "He's here."

An icy wave of cold tore through the tent, making all three of the cousins shiver. Robby took a second to try and calm himself down.

"We want to know more about you," Robby said. He did his best to try and sound like the paranormal investigators he'd seen on *Ghost Talkers* and *Spirit Sleuths*. "Will you communicate with us again?"

"Yes," John said. His voice was airy as if the cold wind itself was blowing through the earbuds.

"He'll talk to us," Robby whispered, keeping his cousins in the loop.

"Find out who Helen is," Michelle whispered.

"I'll try." *Like I wasn't going to ask that?* Robby thought irritatedly.

"John, you mentioned that you're still here because of someone named Helen."

"She's close by," John said.

Robby shuddered. Hearing a ghost talk directly to him was one thing. Having a ghost say that someone he was looking for was close somehow seemed even more terrifying.

"What did he say, Robby?" Ty asked. He had half of his face covered with his pillow, like he was going to hide behind it at any moment.

Robby held up a finger to keep Ty quiet for a second.

"We don't know who Helen is, John," Robby said quickly. "Can you tell us—"

"Where are you?"

It was John, but Robby didn't think the question was directed at him.

"It's like he's calling to her or something," Robby whispered to his cousins. "I still don't know who she is, though. It's like he's not listening to me."

"I came home, and you weren't there," John said. His voice sounded faint and Robby began to worry that the spirit was running out of strength again.

"Was Helen your wife?"

"I came home . . . I promised you I'd be okay."

Robby looked at the shadow outside their tent. Instead of just standing there, John seemed to be taking a few steps back and forth as if pacing. He seemed agitated and confused.

"What's happening?" Michelle asked.

Both hers and Ty's faces looked terrified, washed pale white in the moonlight.

"He came home, and she wasn't there," Robby whispered quickly. "I don't know where he was, though."

"I need to find her," John insisted. The strength of his voice was fading each time he said anything.

Robby saw that the shadow seemed hazier too. He knew that it wouldn't be long until John was gone again.

They were running out of time.

"My tour is over," John said. *"I know you worried about me."*

Something inside Robby clicked just then.

"What year is it, John?" Robby asked.

"1918," John whispered faintly.

"Why are you asking him that?" Michelle asked. "What happened to figuring out who Helen is?"

"He thinks it's 1918," Robby whispered. He didn't know if John could hear him. As strange as it sounded, he didn't want to offend the ghost.

"What?" Michelle cried, her voice still caught in a frightened whisper. "That's like a hundred years ago!"

Robby shook his head as if to say he didn't understand either.

"Where were you, John?" Robby asked quickly. "Why were you away from home?"

There was no answer. Robby looked up to where the shadow had stood outside their tent. John had disappeared.

"He's gone," Robby said, pointing to the tent wall.

Both Michelle and Ty turned to look. The shadowy figure was replaced by the shadow of the dead branches of the nearby tree.

"What else did he say?" Michelle asked. "Not that I want to know. This whole thing has me seriously creeped out."

"He followed us here," Ty whispered. "To the cabin!"

"I know, I know," Robby said. "He said something that didn't make much sense to me."

They all looked down at his phone.

"You were recording the whole time, right?" Michelle asked.

"Yeah," Robby said. "I was."

He stopped recording and played the video back.

With a quick tug, he pulled the earbuds from his ears and the cord from the bottom of his smartphone.

They listened to John tell him he'd talk to them and seemingly ignore the question about who Helen was. Michelle shook her head when she heard the ghost say he thought it was the year 1918.

"Wait," she said. "What did he say before that?"

"Something about a tour," Robby said. "Like the museum tour, I guess? I don't know."

"Play it back," Michelle ordered. She was craning her neck in an attempt to help her hear better.

"My tour is over," John said.

"No way," Michelle said.

"What?" Ty asked. "What does it mean?"

"First off, he wasn't talking about taking the museum tour," Michelle said. "There's no way the museum was even there then."

"You're right," Robby said. "I think I saw something that said the first bus was in operation around 1914. They wouldn't have a museum for something that was only four years old."

"Right," Michelle said. "So, he wasn't talking about that kind of tour."

Ty looked confused. He looked to both Robby and Michelle to explain what they'd figured out.

"He's talking about a tour of duty," Robby said.

"That's right," Michelle said. "John was away from home because he was a soldier."

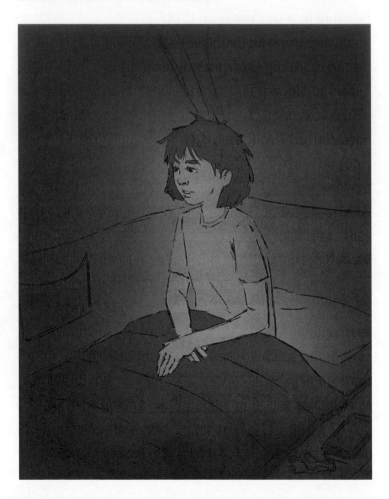

CHAPTER 9

DIGGING INTO THE PAST

Robby could practically feel the wheels spinning inside his head. He thought of a bunch of different scenarios and possibilities to explain what happened to John and who the mysterious Helen might be.

"He thinks it's 1918," Michelle said. "What war was happening back then?"

Robby felt like he should know the answer but wasn't exactly sure. "World War II? Or was it the first one?"

He grabbed his phone and flipped to a search window. The internet wasn't strong near the cabin, but he had a few bars worth of connectivity.

He typed "War 1918" into the search app.

"World War I," Robby said, reading back the very first entry. "It actually ended in 1918."

They all let that sink in a moment as Robby glanced at the tent wall, half expecting to see John's shadow hovering in the moonlight once again. His ghost was long gone.

"So, let's think about this," Michelle said. "John goes off to fight in the war for who knows how long. He has someone named Helen waiting for him to come back. The war ends, and he's sent back home."

Robby watched his cousin. She had a faraway look in her eye as if she were seeing the story unfold right in front of her. It was almost like watching a police detective put together a case using the few clues she had.

"So, he takes the bus back here to Hibbing, right?" Ty offered.

"Yeah," Michelle says. "This is probably where he lived."

Robby looked down at the phone in his hand. He tried to imagine what it was like back then. There were no such things as text messages or the internet. His grandpa always talked about how he missed the day when people wrote letters and talked to each other face-to-face.

Back then, they didn't have a choice, Robby thought.

"So, he gets home and Helen, whoever she is, isn't there," Robby said. "To him it's like she's vanished or something."

But it didn't make sense. *How could someone, especially in a small town like Hibbing, Minnesota, just disappear?*

"What do you guys think happened?" Ty whispered. He was clutching his sleeping bag. The look on his face made it seem like he wasn't sure he actually wanted his question answered.

Robby shrugged.

"I wonder what Hibbing was like in 1918," Michelle said. "Can I see your phone for a second?"

Robby handed it over and watched as Michelle typed in a few things.

"Okay," she said. "That's weird."

Robby knew he wouldn't even have to ask what she'd found. She was going to tell them no matter what.

"They moved the town of Hibbing back then," Michelle said. "Like, all 188 buildings of it."

Robby and Ty both spoke at the same time.

"Huh?" Robby asked.

Ty asked, "What? How can they move the whole town?"

Then he gasped.

"Maybe that's what happened," Ty cried. "John got

back to Hibbing and it wasn't there anymore. The entire town disappeared!"

Robby thought that seemed a little crazy. "I don't think that's—"

"No," Michelle said. "Cool theory, though. They didn't start moving the town until 1919. That's a year after John came back from the war, right?"

"Well, he didn't say that's when he came back," Robby said. "He just thinks it's 1918 now and he can't find Helen."

"Oh," Ty said. "Well, it was an idea."

"Totally," Robby said. "And considering we have no idea where or who Helen is, no ideas are bad ones."

"Why would they have to move the town?" Ty asked. "That seems really weird to me."

Michelle ran her thumb along the side of the screen, scrolling down through the article.

"I guess Hibbing was a mining town then," she said, reading. "They built the original city on top of a big iron ore deposit. Since they needed a lot of metal for the war, they decided to relocate Hibbing two miles south to a little community called Alice."

"There's a place once known as Alice, but we can't figure out who Helen is," Robby mused. "It really gets weird in Minnesota, the farther north you go."

Michelle looked up from the phone for a moment as if trying to digest everything she'd read in the articles.

"So, John gets home, and he can't find Helen anywhere. Then a year or so later, they decide to shift Hibbing so it's no longer on top of valuable iron ore deposits," Michelle says.

"It's weird, though," Robby said. "Did John die in 1918? Or is he stuck on that date because that's when he lost track of Helen?"

He thought back to the paranormal shows he'd watched. A lot of times ghosts lingered around in the real world because they had unfinished business or unanswered questions. Robby considered that maybe

John returned to the time when he originally couldn't find her.

Was he so upset by Helen going missing that when he died his soul couldn't find peace? Robby wondered if he'd ever know. While they were able to talk to John's ghost, he didn't always have complete answers. And he often seemed distracted too.

Robby reached for his phone and Michelle steered it away from him.

"Just a sec," she said, turning her attention to it. "I want to look at one more thing."

"Why aren't we using your phone?" Robby asked.

"It's dead," Michelle said, then cringed. "Sorry, John."

Robby watched as she looked up "Hibbing Map 1918."

"What are you thinking you'll find?" he asked, then watched as Michelle scrolled through a few of the maps but didn't seem to find what she was looking for.

"I wanted to see if the graveyard by the bus museum was there in 1918. What's the name of that place?"

"Oh!" Ty said and raised his hand like he was in class. "I know! It's Hibbing Park Cemetery."

Both Michelle and Robby looked at their younger cousin.

"How do you know that?" Robby asked.

"There was a sign," Ty said, shrugging. "How else?"

Searching "Hibbing Park Cemetery," this time, Michelle found a handful of articles and scrolled through. As she did, she stopped on one. Robby leaned in closer and saw that it showed the year 1918, the name of the cemetery, and Hibbing.

"Uh oh," Michelle said.

She pointed to two words included in the article: "yellow fever."

"There was a camp for people who had yellow fever back in 1918," Michelle said. "They packed everyone who was sick into these tents to try and take care of them."

Robby felt his ears ring as things started to come together in his head.

"Where was the camp?" Robby asked, pretty much already knowing the answer.

"Right next door to the cemetery," Michelle said. "I think they put it there so that when people died of the fever, they were near the graveyard to dispose of the bodies. Oh, that's awful."

Robby exhaled.

"And what's on the site where the quarantine camp used to be?" Robby asked.

Michelle looked at him and nodded.

"The museum," the both said together.

Ty seemed confused until Michelle showed him a sketched map of where the quarantine camp was back in 1918 and where the Hibbing Bus Museum is now.

"They built a museum on top of a place where a bunch of people died?" Ty asked, much louder than Robby expected.

"Please go to sleep!" someone in one of the neighboring tents shouted at them.

Both Robby and Michelle shushed him.

"Sorry," Ty whispered.

"So, yeah," Robby said quietly. "It looks like the museum is smack dab on top of where the yellow fever camp used to be."

Michelle read a little more to herself. From time to time, she shook her head.

"If a bunch of people around here died from yellow fever, it was a pretty good place for the camp," she said.

"Yeah," Robby said. "Nice and convenient."

Reading some more, they discovered that the cemetery wasn't "officially" in use until 1919. Though there wasn't any proof, some historians believe they buried the people who died from yellow fever there.

"Maybe that's why they decided to just turn it into

a graveyard," Robby said. "It was already being used like one anyway."

"Who knows," Michelle said. "But, ugh. I've read enough."

She tossed the phone back to Robby, who set it on his sleeping bag.

The three of them sat in in the semi-darkness with the sound of every cricket in existence chirping the night away.

Robby let his mind wander. He didn't want to say out loud what he was thinking. He was pretty sure Ty was going to have enough trouble falling asleep.

Who knows how many ghosts are wandering around that museum? Martha at the museum told us about the little girl. We saw a shadow make the door open. Maybe that wasn't John after all. It could be any number of the poor souls that died from yellow fever back in 1918.

"I wish we could do something to help John," Ty whispered. Robby looked to see his cousin was resting his head on his pillow. "He seems frustrated and lost."

Robby nodded. "If we only knew who Helen was."

Michelle climbed back onto her air mattress and slipped back into her sleeping bag.

"I mean, she's got to be his wife or girlfriend or something, right?" she replied. "He's off at war, comes back after who knows what horrible things he saw, and discovers that she's disappeared."

"You think it's possible she ran away or something?" Robby asked.

"Who knows?" Michelle let out a long sigh. "Maybe she didn't want to wait around for him. Maybe she met someone else and left poor John on his own."

"Maybe she had the fever too," Ty suggested.

The idea was like a bowling ball to Robby's stomach. They were so worked up about a mass grave and possible ghosts that no one stopped to think that maybe Helen got sick and died too.

"That's a really good possibility, Ty," Robby said. "Wow."

Michelle sat up. "Are you sure you're only ten?"

Robby laughed. "You're eleven, Michelle. It's not like you're that much older than he is."

"Whatever," she said. "Not like you being twelve is that much older than me."

Robby lay down on his pillow and tugged his sleeping bag up toward his neck. He watched the branches dance back and forth in the moonlight and tried not to think about the shadow standing outside their tent just a little while ago. Though he didn't think John would

hurt them, the thought of someone dead watching them made him shiver a bit.

"We should go back," Robby said finally.

"The museum is closed tomorrow, genius," Michelle said. "Fourth of July."

"Not back to the museum," Robby said. "Back to the graveyard."

Michelle hid her face underneath the sleeping bag and groaned, letting the thick fabric muffle the sound.

"What are we going to do, Robby?" Ty asked.

"We're going to help John find Helen," Robby replied.

CHAPTER 10

ALL TOGETHER

Robby, Michelle, and Ty were up early on the Fourth of July. They each wolfed down a bowl of cereal, hopped on their antique bicycles, and rode off for the Hibbing Park Cemetery before anyone else was awake.

After riding for nearly a half hour, they turned off 3rd Avenue and onto one of the dirt roads that led into the graveyard. A light mist hung over the ground, giving the already damp grass a hazy look.

"It's like riding onto the set of a horror movie," Michelle said.

They hopped off their bikes and parked them near a large oak tree about fifty yards in.

Robby scanned the graveyard as if trying to figure out where to start.

"So, what do we do, Robby?" Ty asked.

"Well," Robby began, nodding a little as if to encourage himself. "I think we start looking. We can check gravestones for anyone named 'Helen' and see if we can get John to see it."

Michelle crossed her arms and cocked her head a bit.

"You think that's going to work?" she asked. "What if John can't actually see what we're trying to show him?"

Robby turned to face his cousin.

"He was standing outside our tent last night," Robby reminded her. "I think he can see us and the rest of the living world."

"Good point," Michelle replied.

Ty was already wandering over to some flat stones set into the ground. He read one to himself then moved to the next one. Though it wasn't an enormous cemetery, it was a decent size for a relatively small town in Northern Minnesota. It wasn't going to go quickly.

"This is going to take forever," Robby said, looking out over the horizon.

"I found a Helen," Ty announced.

Robby felt his spirits lift immediately and he and Michelle ran over to where Ty was. He couldn't believe how lucky they were to find her right away.

This is it. Now we'll know who Helen is and maybe what she meant to John!

"Oh," Ty said. "Sorry. Never mind. This Helen was born in 1974 and died in 2005."

Robby looked down at the stone. It was relatively newer looking in contrast to some of the older ones peppered across the field of grass.

"Yeah, that's not her," he said. "Good eye, though."

"Okay, let's not do that anymore," Michelle said. "I'm guessing there are going to be a handful of Helens out here, right? Seems like kind of an older name."

"True," Robby said. "Maybe we should split up. If you spot a Helen, look at the dates and see if it makes sense. If so, call us over."

"And keep an eye out for John, too, right?" Ty asked.

"Yeah," Robby said. "You see something weird, shout."

With a plan in place, they moved in opposite directions. They did their best to stay relatively close so that they could keep an eye on each other.

Robby plugged one of his earbuds in and made a constant video of the gravestones as he walked by them. He saw names from long ago: Albert, Chester, Beatrice, Myra. Many of the stones were dark with age, others were covered in moss.

The ones he could see were clearly not Helen, he moved on from.

As he walked along, he saw a flat stone overgrown with grass. It was partially covered in dirt, but the letter

"H" could be seen. Robby squatted down to clear it away and felt an instant rush of cold drift over him. He knew well enough by then that it wasn't the mist or a change in the weather.

John was nearby.

"Am I close, John?" Robby asked. "Is this Helen?"

There was no answer, making him wonder if he had to play the video back like they did in the bus museum.

But first, Robby used his free hand to dig away at the clumps of grass and dirt that collected on top of the stone. After a little work, he uncovered the next letter.

E.

This has got to be it. I think I've found her grave!

With a great tug, he uncovered the rest of the gravestone. He sighed when he read the name at his feet.

"Herman," Robby whispered. *Not Helen.*

He brushed the dirt from his hand off onto his shorts. He stood up before looking to see where his cousins were at. Robby hadn't heard a peep from either of them and wondered if they were feeling as discouraged as he was.

Are we just wasting our time out here? Even if we find Helen's grave, assuming it's here, then what?

Robby continued to search the graveyard but had no

luck. Michelle found two more Helens but they didn't seem to fit within the timeline they were looking for. Ty said all the markers he'd found were newer ones.

After another forty-five minutes, they'd covered the entire graveyard.

"I think that's all of them," Michelle said. "I don't think Helen is out here."

"We should head back, then," Ty said. "We've got fireworks to watch."

"Yeah, okay," Robby said. "But they're not doing fireworks until it's much darker, Ty."

"I know, I know," Ty mumbled.

As the trio headed back toward their bikes, something caught Robby's eye. Along the tree line that separated the bus museum from the graveyard was an overgrown patch of grass. He stopped and stared, squinting in the sun to see if he could make out what it was.

He decided to jog over to check it out.

"Hey!" Michelle shouted. "I thought we were going back!"

"Just a minute," Robby called. "I want to see something!"

As he got closer to the tree line, he could hear the

footfalls of Michelle and Ty running toward him. When they were all together, Michelle shivered.

"It's cold over here," she said, rubbing her arms.

"It's John," Robby said. "I think he's here."

"Where is she?" John's whispery voice came through Robby's earbuds.

Robby sucked in his breath. He had forgotten that he was still recording and didn't expect to hear the ghost's voice.

"What's wrong?" Ty asked.

"John just asked me where she is," Robby said, struggling to catch his breath. "I wasn't expecting that."

Robby crept closer to the edge of the trees. Through the branches and tree trunks, he could see the museum. Some of the other buses that wouldn't fit into the interior display were out around the back.

"What're we looking for?" Ty asked.

Robby looked down at his feet. Mostly hidden beneath the long, unmown grass was a small flat stone in the ground. Instinctively, Robby crouched down and began to clear the grass and dirt from the top of it.

The stone felt cool to the touch and Robby wasn't sure if it was because of the shade from the trees or the moisture in the ground. When he brushed the torn grass clippings and leaves away, he read the inscription aloud.

"Mass grave," Robby said. "In this place, many un-named victims of the Yellow Fever epidemic of 1918 are buried. Known only to God, may they find peace."

"What?" Ty asked, quietly, almost stammering. "What does that mean?"

Michelle blew the air from her mouth like someone preparing to give bad news.

"I think it means there are a whole bunch of un-identified people who died from yellow fever buried here," Michelle said. "As they died, they probably took them from the quarantine camp and put them here."

Robby nodded. "Makes sense that it would be close," he added.

"That's terrible," Ty whispered. "All in the same grave? No names?"

"She's close," John said in Robby's ear. *"I can feel her."*

Robby stood up. It made the back of his neck prickle, knowing there were nameless bodies buried where they stood. He didn't know if it would work, but he had an idea.

"Helen?" Robby called. "Are you here?"

Nothing happened. The wind blew through the trees and a car passed on 3rd Avenue, heading into down-town Hibbing.

"John is looking for you, Helen," Robby said quietly. "He wants to know where you are."

Michelle looked at Robby like he had a screw loose.

"Do you think she's in there, Robby?" Ty asked. "In this big grave?"

"I don't know," Robby admitted. "For all we know, she could be anywhere."

I wonder how many people died from the yellow fever outbreak?

The air got a little colder.

"Helen," John whispered.

A small dark hand emerged from the ground, followed by a head. Robby and his cousins watched as a small shadowy figure seemed to climb out of the mass grave, right before their eyes.

"It's a little girl," Michelle said. It sounded like she was out of breath.

Robby nodded, almost stunned and frozen into place. As he watched, the shadow began to materialize from a shadow to a blurry form that resembled a little girl.

Is this the little girl other people have reported seeing in the museum? Was it Helen all along?

To his left, a taller shadow figure appeared. It looked as tall as the one they'd seen outside their tent the night before. Like the little girl, John's form began to change. It went from looking like a dark shadow to an image of

a young man. Though hazy, Robby could see that John was wearing a military uniform, the kind soldiers wore in public.

They all watched as the two spirits met for what may have been the first time in one hundred years. John stepped forward and opened his arms. Helen fell into him, accepting his hug.

"Helen wasn't his wife," Robby whispered.

"She was his little sister," Michelle finished his thought.

Ty watched quietly in stunned fascination.

"Where were you?" John asked. *"I came home and couldn't find you."*

"I got sick, Johnny," Helen replied. Her voice lighter and airier, the voice of a child.

The cousins watched as the ghost siblings broke away from their hug. John held Helen's hand in his and they stood there, looking at each other for a moment.

"Sorry, John," Robby said. "I'm sorry about what happened to your sister."

The ghostly soldier turned to Robby and his cousins and seemed to nod.

"Thank you," he said.

Helen tugged at her big brother's hand, as if trying to lead him away from the living.

"C'mon, Johnny," she said. *"It's time to go home."*

And before they knew it, John and his little sister took a few steps toward the trees and disappeared into the July sunlight as if they were never there.

The silence that followed was almost thick enough to cut with a knife.

"Holy wow," Michelle gasped, finally. "I can't even believe that just happened."

Robby could only shake his head in disbelief. His whole body felt like it was electrified with a mixture of relief and adrenaline. He looked down at his phone, still recording and saw how badly his hand was shaking.

He pressed STOP and wondered if he'd succeeded in recording the ground or if he caught any of the ghostly encounter on his phone. It didn't matter.

"That's what was keeping him here on Earth," Robby said. "Not ever knowing what happened to his little sister."

"Yeah," Ty replied. "I guess he couldn't rest until he found her."

Robby looked at his younger cousin. "I just realized something, Ty," Robby said. "You guessed the little girl everyone was seeing in the museum might've been Helen all along. We should've listened to you."

Michelle stepped forward and Ty seemed to brace himself for a smart aleck comment.

"You did good, Ty," Michelle said and clapped him on the shoulder.

Ty smiled a little and Robby could see he was a bit embarrassed.

"Thanks. It was just a lucky guess," he said and shrugged a little.

They all stood quiet for a moment. Robby looked down at the stone that marked the mass grave. He wondered how many other spirits were stuck in the living world, looking for the spirits of the forgotten laid to rest below them.

We did what we could.

"You think John and Helen are gone for good now, Robby?" Ty asked. "Like at rest or whatever?"

"It feels like it," Robby said. And it did. The cold and heavy feeling that John seemed to have brought with him seemed to have completely vanished.

"I think so too," Ty said.

"Hey, enough standing around. We should get back to our own family reunion," Michelle said. "What do you guys say?"

Together, the three of them hopped back onto their

classic bikes and raced toward Uncle Stewart's cabin. Robby felt lighter than he had since they first stepped into the bus museum. On the way back to their family, he was even tempted to pull his bike's stick shift one more time. But he decided not to.

AUTHOR'S NOTE

It's always fun to write a story that takes place in the state where I grew up. Though I've lived in Minnesota all my life, I've never been to Hibbing where *Ghostly Reunion* takes place. But hearing that there could be a haunted bus museum there makes me want to visit!

The parts about the bus windows opening and closing on their own are from actual reports from people who have witnessed paranormal happenings in Hibbing's bus museum. There are also reports of shadows moving between the buses and down the aisles of some buses.

I decided to not make the little girl the main ghost in this book. Although many people, including Hibbing police officers, have claimed to see her, I wanted to try something different. I was inspired by a photo of a bunch of mannequins near one of the buses. All of them looked like soldiers or their loved ones, seeing them board the bus to go off to war. I thought it might be interesting to have a soldier return home to find that someone very special to him was no longer there. So, in a sense, I tried to combine the shadow figures people see with the little girl.

While the bus museum is based on a real place, Tooty the cartoon bus character is a work of fiction. I wanted to have something old and creepy from that era to scare Robby and his cousins.

So why is the bus museum haunted? Some truly believe it is because so many died on the site because of the yellow fever outbreak. Others think that when Hibbing was relocated (also a true story!) that they used dirt from a former hospital to fill in areas around the museum. Or maybe it really is just because their closest neighbor is a cemetery. Whatever the reason, you should stop in to see some buses and maybe a ghost or two. All aboard!

ABOUT THE AUTHOR

Thomas Kingsley Troupe has been making up stories ever since he was in short pants. As an "adult," he's the author of a whole lot of books for kids. When he's not writing, he enjoys movies, biking, taking naps, and investigating ghosts as a member of the Twin Cities Paranormal Society. Raised in "Nordeast" Minneapolis, he now lives in Woodbury, Minnesota, with his awe-inspiring family.

ABOUT THE ILLUSTRATOR

Maggie Ivy is a freelance illustrator and artist who lives and works in the Ozark area in Arkansas. She found her love for art at an early age and pursued it with passion. She graduated from The Florence Academy of Art in 2010. She loves narrative elements and story-building moments, and seeks to implement them in her own work.

A TENNESSEE GHOST STORY

Miles Watley is pretty sure he's going to die of boredom when his family moves to the small town of Adams, Tennessee. The only thing that is remotely interesting to him is the Bell Witch Cave that local lore claims is haunted. While exploring the cave, he and his brother, Ryder, spot a young girl who simply vanishes into the darkness. Shortly after, weird, ghostly things start happening in his family's new house, the most perplexing of which is Ryder's strange behavior and his dad's mysterious illness. It becomes clear that the Watleys have something the ghost wants. It isn't their house, is it?